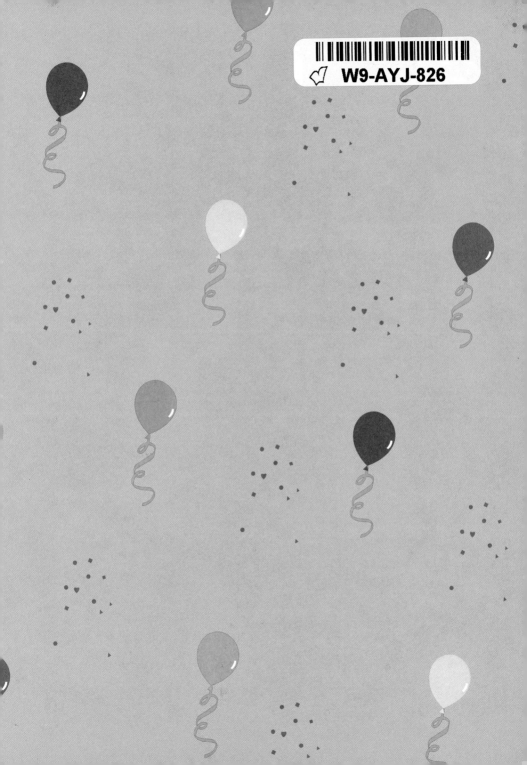

BIRTHDAY PARTY ™

by Effin Older

DUALSTAR PUBLICATIONS PARACHUTE PRESS

SCHOLASTIC INC.
New York   Toronto   London   Auckland   Sydney

DUALSTAR PUBLICATIONS PARACHUTE PRESS

Dualstar Publications
c/o 10100 Santa Monica Blvd.
Suite 2200
Los Angeles, CA 90067

Parachute Press, Inc.
156 Fifth Avenue
Suite 325
New York, NY 10010

Published by Scholastic Inc.

With special thanks to Robert Thorne and Harold Weitzberg.

Printed in the U.S.A.
March 1998
ISBN: 0-590-22593-6
A B C D E F G H I J

"Mmmm!" My sister Ashley licked frosting off her finger. "I love birthday cake. Especially when it's for *my* birthday!"

"Me too!" I agreed. I slapped high fives with Ashley.

I'm Mary-Kate Olsen. Ashley and I share the same birthday—because we're twins. We both have strawberry blond hair and big, blue eyes.

We look alike. But we don't always think alike.

A couple of days ago, we started to plan our birthday celebration. Ashley wanted to have a big party with all our friends.

But I told her I wanted a small party with just our family.

We had two totally different ideas! And one *big* problem!

"A small party with Mom, Dad, Lizzie, and Trent would be the most fun," I told Ashley.

Lizzie is our little sister. She's six. Trent is our big brother. He's eleven.

"But Trent can be a real pain when he teases us," Ashley said. "And Lizzie is a pain when she wants to do everything we do."

"They won't do that at our birthday party," I told her. "Remember how much fun we had at our family party last year?"

"*Hmmm.* It *was* fun singing and playing games with Trent and Lizzie," Ashley said. "Okay, Mary-Kate. A family party it is!"

Pssst!

I knew something Ashley didn't know. She was about to be totally surprised! Because...

We weren't going to have a family party at all! I was really planning a *surprise* party—for Ashley! I sent special invitations to our friends Jill, Belinda, and Lisa. "It will be the best birthday party ever!" I wrote.

Now it was the day of our party. Our friends would be here any minute.

The problem was, they were supposed to meet me in the kitchen. And I had to get Ashley *out* before they arrived!

"I'll finish decorating the cake," I told her. "You go in the backyard and pick some flowers for the table."

"Sounds good to me!" Ashley replied. She ran outside.

But two minutes later she was back!

"Quick, Mary-Kate!" Ashley exclaimed. "Come outside with me!"

"Why?" I asked.

"I have to show you something amazing!" Ashley said.

I glanced nervously at the clock. Our friends were coming any second. I had to be in the kitchen to meet them—alone. Or my big surprise would be totally ruined!

"I *can't* go!" I said. "Uh, I have to finish the cake."

"But you *have* to come outside," Ashley begged. "It's really, really important!"

This sounded serious. But what could be so important?

I followed Ashley to the backyard.

"Wow!" I exclaimed. I stared around, totally confused. "Who put up all these really cool decorations?"

Brightly colored balloons hung from the trees and the fence.

More balloons hung in a huge arch over the swimming pool.

Before Ashley could answer, Lisa, Belinda, and Jill jumped out from behind a tree.

"Surprise!" they all shouted together.

Lisa, Belinda, and Jill laughed out loud.

"Wha...what are you guys doing out here?" I asked. "You were supposed to meet me in the kitchen!"

"What are you talking about?" Belinda asked.

"The party…" I began. Then Ashley interrupted me.

"They're here for your party!" she shouted. "A *surprise* birthday pool party—for you!"

I couldn't believe it! A surprise party for *me*?

"This is amazing!" I said, grinning at Ashley. "I planned a surprise party for *you*, too!"

Ashley burst out laughing. "I guess this is one time that we did think exactly alike!"

"No, you didn't think *exactly* alike," Jill said. "Mary-Kate, you forgot something really important!"

Oh, no!

"What?" I asked. "What did I forget?"

"You forgot to invite me to Ashley's surprise party!" Jill cried.

"And me," Belinda said.

"And me," Lisa added. "My feelings are hurt!"

My mouth dropped open. "I didn't forget. I sent you all invitations. They were so cute—I wrote them on pink paper."

"Well, I'm glad you sent them." Lisa smiled. "But we never got them!"

"But I put them in the mailbox myself," I said. "What could have happened to them?"

"It doesn't matter," Ashley told me. "We can still have a great time. Let's party! Everyone into the pool!"

"Wait!" I held up my hand. "Not yet!"

Ashley stared at me. "What's wrong?" she asked.

"I have a problem. You planned a pool party," I answered. "But *I* planned a costume party. Now we have to decide which party to have."

"That's easy," Belinda said. "We can have both parties!"

"Sure!" Lisa agreed. "Two parties will be twice the fun!"

"Your problem is solved," Jill added.

"Except for one more little thing," I replied.

"We don't know which party to have first!" I said.

"That's no problem, Mary-Kate," Ashley told me. "I'm two minutes older than you are. Oldest goes first."

"So we'll start with my party for you, right?" I said.

Ashley shook her head. "No. That means we'll start with my party for *you*!"

"All right!" Lisa shouted. "Everybody into the pool!"

Ashley and I quickly changed into our bathing suits and hurried back outside.

"Last one in is a rotten egg!" Lisa yelled.

Jill and I and Ashley and Lisa dived into the water at the exact same time!

"This is great!" Lisa yelled.

Ashley scrambled onto a float. She pretended to be riding the waves. "Look, everybody! I'm surfing!" she shouted.

But our friends weren't paying attention. In fact, they weren't even in the pool! They had all gotten out!

Lisa, Belinda, and Jill were huddled together whispering. They all had worried looks on their faces.

"Hey, you guys," Ashley called. "What's wrong?"

Nobody answered.

Jill was checking under the seats of the lounge chairs. Lisa was unfolding all the towels. And Belinda was peering under one of the potted plants.

"You guys!" I called. "What in the world are you doing?"

"Oh! I was, uh, just admiring your plants," Belinda called. "They're so—so green!"

"I'm shaking out the towels to make sure they're dry!" Lisa added quickly.

"And I'm fluffing up the seats so they'll be extra comfortable," Jill explained. Her cheeks turned bright red.

I climbed up onto a dinosaur float. Ashley scrambled up behind me.

"Our friends are acting a little weird," I whispered.

"You're right. What do you think is going on?" she asked.

"Search me," I replied. "Maybe they're not having a good time in the pool."

Jill whispered something to Belinda and Lisa. Then they dived under the water. I could see them gliding toward us.

I wasn't sure what they were doing before—but now I knew *exactly* what they were up to!

"Look out, Ashley!" I shouted.

Too late!

The dinosaur float lifted beneath us—and Ashley and I tumbled into the water!
SPLOOOOOSH!

We smiled at our friends smiling underwater.

"I know! Let's play underwater tag!" Lisa shouted. "Jill, you're it!"

We played tag for awhile. Then Ashley poked me. "Everyone seems happy now," she said. "Do you think they're having fun?"

"I think so," I started to say. But before I could finish, a loud scream filled the air!

It was someone shouting, "CANNONBALL!"

Two boys in bathing suits raced through our backyard gate. They charged toward the pool.

"Oh, no!" I cried. "It's Trent's friends—Eric and Jamie from next door. They are major pains!"

"Double-major pains!" Ashley added. "And they're going to do a cannonball—right into the middle of our party!"

SPLASH!

"What are you doing?" I yelled at the boys.

"You weren't invited to this party," Ashley added.

"Yes, we were," Jamie said. He pointed to his wet bathing suit. "Like my costume?" He smirked. "We're dressed as swimmers—ha, ha!"

Eric held out a piece of soggy pink paper.

It was one of my costume party invitations!

"We found it on the ground in our backyard," Eric said.

I stared at the invitation. There was a muddy pawprint in one corner.

I groaned. "I must have forgotten to close the mailbox door," I said. "The invitations fell out—and then I bet Clue picked them up and tried to bury them in Jamie and Eric's yard!"

Clue is our basset hound. She loves to chew bits of paper and then bury them.

Ashley tapped my shoulder. "What are we going to do?" she whispered. "Eric and Jamie will ruin the party!"

I frowned. "Finding an invitation doesn't count," I told Eric and Jamie. "This party is for us and our friends—not you."

"We can stay if we want to," Jamie said.

I suddenly had an idea. "Sure you can," I said with a grin. "But I hope you like wearing a dress!"

Eric turned red. "A dress! I'd never wear a dress."

"Then you'd better leave," Ashley said. "Because it's time for us to change into our costumes."

"We're going to take pictures and make a birthday scrapbook," I added. "And we have special dresses for you and Jamie to wear!"

"No way!" Eric and Jamie raced out of the backyard.

Lisa, Jill, and Belinda slapped Ashley and me high fives.

"That was great," Lisa told me. "But I didn't know about your party, Mary-Kate. So I didn't bring a costume."

"Me either." Jill looked worried.

"Me either!" Belinda said. "What are we going to do?"

"No problem," I said. "I have great costumes for everybody! Come back into the house and look."

Everybody followed me back into the kitchen.

"Uh, wait a minute," Jill said. "I'm starved! You guys go change. I'll…uh… I'll stay here and find myself a snack."

"A snack?" Ashley said. "I know the perfect snack—birthday cake! And Mary-Kate and I made a great one!"

We sang "Happy Birthday." Then Ashley served chocolate cake to everybody. We ate until we were stuffed.

"You know what comes after the cake, don't you? Opening the presents!" Lisa shouted.

"No!" Jill yelled.

Ashley and I stared at Jill. Jill looked shocked. Belinda seemed surprised. Lisa clapped her hands over her mouth. "Sorry, Jill," she muttered.

"Sorry for what?" I asked.

"Uh, sorry I was so rude," Lisa said. "But you can't open presents yet. Because...um..."

"Because we haven't had your costume party yet!" Belinda finished. "Opening presents should come last."

I shrugged. "Okay. Ashley and I will change first. Then you take our pictures—and try to guess what we are!"

Ashley and I ran into the playroom. I had put all kinds of fun costumes into a big trunk.

We pulled on colorful vests. Ashley picked up a set of noisemakers. She shook them hard. "Maracas!" she cried.

Ashley and I stuck fake mustaches under our noses. We put on big hats. Then I grabbed a trumpet and blew a piercing note. "Come on in!"

Our friends ran into the playroom. "What are we?" I asked.

"Bullfighters?" Belinda guessed.

"Spanish farmers?" Lisa guessed.

"Wrong," Ashley replied. "What's your guess, Jill?"

There was no answer.

Ashley frowned. "Hey, what happened to Jill? She was just here a minute ago!"

"Here I am!" Jill raced back into the playroom. "Hey, cool! You're dressed as Mexican cowboys!"

We grinned. "You guessed right!" Ashley said.

Belinda snapped our pictures.

"Okay. See if you can guess what we are next," I said.

Ashley and I quickly changed into white jackets and tall, puffy white hats.

"Can you *cook up* an answer?" I joked.

"You look exactly like French chefs!" Lisa cried. She snapped her fingers. "Thinking about cooking has made me hungry again. I need another helping of that cake!"

Lisa raced out of the playroom. Belinda and Jill followed her.

"Now they're *all* gone!" I shook my head. "They're acting really weird, Ashley! Do you think they're mad because I messed up the invitations?"

"That doesn't make sense," Ashley told me. "This is silly. Let's just go ask them!"

Ashley and I headed for the door. But before we got there, Belinda and Jill burst back into the play-room.

"What are you doing?" Jill cried. "You can't go out there!"

"We wanted to talk to you guys," Ashley said.

"We can talk in here!" Belinda said.

"But we want to talk to Lisa, too," I told her.

"She's—uh—calling her mom on the phone," Jill said. "I know. Let's try on more costumes while we wait for her!"

I put on a short ice-skating dress. Ashley wore a soccer uniform. "Heads up!" she hollered.

Next, Ashley pulled on a tennis skirt and grabbed a racket. I smeared black grease under my eyes and put on a football outfit.

"Go out for a long pass!" I shouted.

We took pictures of each other. Then Ashley headed for the door again. "I'll go see if Lisa is off the phone," she said.

"No! Wait!" Belinda cried. "Uh—I'll go."

"I'll go, too," Jill said quickly. "You guys wait here."

Before we could say anything, they were gone.
Ashley and I stared at each other.

"Come on," I said. "Let's find out what's *really*
going on!"

Ashley and I crept to the door. I pressed my ear against it.

"Listen!" I whispered.

We could hear Jill, Lisa, and Belinda arguing behind the door.

"I can't believe you lost it, Jill!" Belinda said.

"And I know that Mary-Kate and Ashley think something is wrong," Lisa added.

"If only we could find it!" Jill exclaimed. She sounded close to tears.

"Lost what?" I whispered to Ashley.

"Find what?" she whispered back.

"Don't cry, Jill," we heard Lisa say.

"I can't help it!" Jill let out a sob. "I lost our special birthday present for Mary-Kate and Ashley—right in their own house! Now we have nothing to give them!"

"Are you sure you lost it by the pool?" Belinda asked.

"I don't know," Jill replied. "When I hung up my backpack on a chair I saw the present inside. But then I noticed a hole in the bottom of my backpack. The present must have fallen out!"

Ashley stared at me in surprise. I stared back.

"They lost our birthday present!" I declared.

"That's why they keep running around like crazy. They're trying to find it!" Ashley said.

She frowned. "I feel badly for Jill," she added.

"Me too," I agreed. "How can we make her feel better?"

"I know," Ashley said. "Let's dress Clue up in a costume." She pulled a green doctor's cap and gown out of the trunk and dressed Clue in it.

"Doesn't she look funny?" Ashley asked.

"Yes. Clue does look funny," Ashley said. "But Jill is going to need more than Dr. Clue to cheer her up. We could help her look for the lost present," she suggested.

"No, we can't. We don't know what to look for!" I told her.

Ashley sighed. "You're right. I guess we'd better try on more costumes while our friends look for it."

"Okay," I said. "We'll pretend we still don't know what they're doing. That will give them more time to find it."

Ashley and I pulled on silver astronaut suits. We put big plastic helmets on our heads.

Just then the playroom door opened. Our friends walked back in. All three of them looked unhappy.

"I don't think they found the present," Ashley whispered.

I whispered back, "Then there's only one thing left to do."

"Earth to our friends!" I called out. "This is Captain Mary-Kate Olsen! Co-captain Ashley and I have an important announcement!"

"We know you lost our birthday present," I told them.

"Oh, no!" Jill cried. "We didn't want you to find out."

"It's okay," I said. "I lost your invitations. So I guess we're even."

Jill seemed to feel a little better. "I'd still like to find your present," she said.

"Maybe we can help you," Ashley told her. "We can search the whole house."

"But I know it was in my backpack by the pool," Jill replied.

"Are you sure?" Belinda asked.

Jill frowned at her. "Yes! I told you a hundred times." She looked as if she might cry again.

"Earth to friends!" I repeated. "Don't argue. The present isn't that important."

"Yeah!" Ashley agreed. "Being with all of you on our birthday is what's important. We just want you to have fun."

"And that's an order!" I added.

"I don't think I'll ever have fun again." Jill looked more upset than before.

"Oh, yes, you will," I said. "If you just reach into this—"

"Our special party costume grab bag!" I yelled. "Try one last costume—and then we'll have a treasure hunt. We'll all hunt for the lost present!"

We all grabbed costumes from the costume trunk.

Ashley and I both changed into colorful mini-dresses. I put on a pair of huge sunglasses. Ashley snapped on an enormous bow-tie.

Our friends chose long feathery scarves, clown noses, and funny hats.

"I'm glad you guys don't mind about the present," Jill said. "Now we really are having fun!"

"It's a great party," Lisa agreed.

"But our present was so special. Tickets to Thousand Thrills Amusement Park!" Jill said.

"Wow! That *is* a great present!" I agreed.

"I wish we knew what happened to them." Belinda sighed. "But we don't have a clue!"

I gasped. "Did you say *clue*? You just gave me an idea!"

I let out the loudest whistle I could.

"Clue!" I shouted. "Here, girl!"

A second later our dog trotted into the room.

"What is that stuck to Clue's collar?" I asked.

I pulled some pieces of paper from under her chin. I held one up to the light.

"Admit one to Thousand Thrills Amusement Park," I read out loud. "These are tickets!"

"That's it!" Jill shrieked. "That's your present!"

"I can't believe Clue found them!" Lisa exclaimed.

"I can," I said. "Clue loves to play with paper!"

"I'm just glad she didn't try to bury the tickets the way she tried to bury our invitations!" Ashley exclaimed.

"I guess the tickets fell out of Jill's backpack…" I began.

"And Clue found them!" Ashley finished. "Good girl!" She threw her arms around Clue and gave her a big hug.

So did Jill, Belinda, and Lisa.

"Thanks for the great tickets," I said. "I always wanted to see Thousand Thrills! Let's pick a day when we can all go."

"I know the perfect day," Jill said. "Today!"

"Today?" I asked. "But we already had two parties today."

"That's true," Jill replied. "But it's only fair."

"What do you mean?" Lisa asked.

"Ashley gave her pool party for Mary-Kate," Jill answered. "And Mary-Kate gave her costume party for Ashley. So now it's our turn to have an amusement park party for both of them!"

Ashley and I cheered. "Thousand Thrills, here we come!"

We arrived at Thousand Thrills Amusement Park in no time.

We slid down water slides, rode the Twister and the Whirlwind, and finished with a ride on the biggest, scariest roller coaster ever...

42

The Cyclone!

"Aaaaahhhh!"

We yelled at the top of our lungs as the car whooshed down. It was totally cool!

"I'm so glad we shared three great parties," Ashley said.

"But the fun isn't over yet," I replied. "I have a special present for you," I told Ashley. "I bought it at the penny arcade."

"That's funny!" Ashley grinned. "I bought you a special present at the penny arcade, too!"

Ashley and I reached into our pockets.

We each pulled out our presents.

Ashley's jaw dropped open.

I stared in surprise.

We both held out beautiful gold necklaces with a double-heart charm!

"I guess we just can't help thinking alike!" I exclaimed.

"And we wouldn't have it any other way," Ashley added.

We gave each other a big hug. Our friends gave us big hugs, too.

"Thanks for inviting us to your surprise party," Jill said.

"You mean, thanks for inviting us to your *two* surprise parties," Belinda corrected.

"You mean, to your three-surprise-parties-in-one," Lisa added.

"It doesn't matter what you call it," I told our friends. "Three parties or one—thanks to you, we had the *best* birthday ever!"

Hi from both of us,

Thanks for coming to our triple surprise birthday party. We hope you had a great time. We sure did! Having good friends along makes every party special!

We hope you like your double-heart keepsake necklace as much as we like ours. Wear it at your next party—and we're sure it will be special, too!

Love,

Ashley Olsen & Mary-Kate Olsen

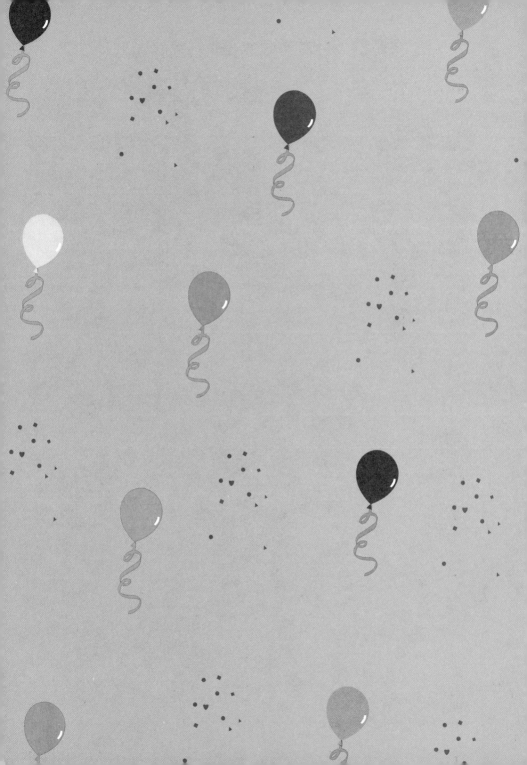